MY AMERICAN JOURNEY

From Settlement to City

with Benjamin Franklin

BY DEBORAH HEDSTROM-PAGE

ILLUSTRATIONS BY SERGIO MARTINEZ

FROM SETTLEMENT TO CITY

© 2007 by B&H Publishing Group

Illustrations © 1997 by Sergio Martinez

All rights reserved.

Printed in Singapore

ISBN: 978-0-8054-3267-1

Published by B&H Publishing Group

Nashville, Tennessee

Dewey Decimal Number: F

Subject Heading: FRANKLIN, BENJAMIN \ UNITED STATES—HISTORY—1776—FICTION \
CONSTITUTIONAL HISTORY—UNITED STATES—FICTION

Unless otherwise stated, all Scripture is taken from the HCSB, Holman Christian Standard Bible™,
copyright 1999, 2000, 2002, 2003 Holman Bible Publishers.

1 2 3 4 5 6 7 8 9 10   11 10 09 08 07

Foreword

Most people think of Benjamin Franklin as a pudgy old man with square glasses and straggly gray hair. They remember that he flew a kite in a storm and took part in the American Revolution. But he did a whole lot more! His ideas and inventions helped change the settlement of Philadelphia into the city of Philadelphia.

From firefighting to electrical batteries, Ben Franklin was always figuring out how to make, improve, and use what surrounded him. All kinds of things captured his attention. He studied ants, earthquakes, wind currents, lightning, ocean water, sunspots, and colors—just to name a few.

He constantly shook up the early American people in Philadelphia with suggestions for how to change and improve things. If he wasn't writing about his ideas in his newspaper, he was arguing for them in the Pennsylvania Assembly.

But even though people often felt frustrated at this man who could never let well-enough alone, they enjoyed Mr. Franklin's humor. From electric kisses to the clever words of his fictional character, Poor Richard, he made them smile, giggle, and laugh right out loud.

In spite of the fun, Ben Franklin caused some people to worry. For a while they didn't know if he just liked clashing and causing trouble or if he was really trying to help the settlement.

The Penn family, who owned the colony of Pennsylvania, wondered which was true. Using a little imagination, we can picture their worry when news of this idea-filled young printer reached them in England. With a little more imagination, we can even create someone who was there with them. Through her eyes, we'll see Ben Franklin's effect on the Penn family in the 1700s—and on the people of Philadelphia and the American colonies. We meet her on the next page. A servant has just shown her into the parlor of Miss Hannah Penn, daughter of the colony's founder, William Penn.

Introduction

Suzanna pretended a book balanced on her head. She sat straight with her chin up, trying to look as if she belonged in the fancy parlor. But anyone could see she didn't. Nervously twisting her handkerchief between her fingers, she wondered for the hundredth time, *Why does Miss Hannah Penn want to see me? Her family owns land in England and the American colonies, and my father simply sells books here in England. The Penns socialize with lords and ladies, not merchants' daughters!*

A rustle of silk interrupted Suzanna's thoughts. A young woman with frail, porcelain-like skin entered the room, her dress sweeping the floor as she walked. She extended her hand to Suzanna. "Welcome to my home, Miss Hale."

A maid followed Hannah Penn into the room carrying a large silver tray that held a teapot and a plate of crumpets. Miss Penn poured a cup of tea then held it out to Suzanna.

Suzanna clutched her teacup with both hands, afraid to sip the hot, steaming drink. She knew if she lifted it, her hands would shake, and she'd spill it for sure.

"Miss Hale, I invited you here today to speak with you of a job. I recently learned that your family is moving to my father's colony in the Americas. I wish you to keep me informed of what's happening there," she said, getting right to the point.

"When my father, William Penn, received this land from the king as payment for a debt, he named it Pennsylvania and made special plans for the colony. As a young child, I often heard him speak of it as a 'holy experiment.' He was a Quaker, as you probably know, and my father wanted followers of this faith and of other religions to have a place to worship freely.

"Twice, he traveled to America, planning the settlement and making peace with the nearby Indians by paying them for the land the king had already given him. He picked a spot next to a big river for the colony's main settlement. He used stakes to mark where the streets, buildings, and parks would be, and he found the best place for a harbor. He told the colonists who sailed from England to settle the land, to call the settlement Philadelphia, which means *brotherly love* in Greek. And he allowed the people to make their own laws and govern themselves."

Miss Penn stopped her story for a moment and pulled her shawl more tightly around her frail shoulders. She got up to stare out a window, continuing in a distracted voice, "My father paid dearly for his dream. It took most of his money, and he ended up in a debtor's prison because he refused to sell the colony and have it be taken over by the king. Recently I found an old letter he wrote to a friend. It said, 'O Pennsylvania, what hast thou not cost me! Thirty thousand pounds more than I ever got from it, two hazardous and most tiring voyages, prison and dire straits.'"

As Suzanna listened, she forgot the imagined book on her head and the teacup nestled in her hands. "Was it worth it? How *is* the colony?" she asked.

"That is what I hope you will find out for me," Miss Hannah continued as she turned around and faced her guest. "I was nine years old when my father died. I did not realize the price he paid to create a free colony. For eighteen years I cared little for his 'holy experiment.' But recently I found his letter, and now I want to know more. My brothers oversee the colony, but they spend most of their time here in England. They share little news of Pennsylvania with me. I desire written records of the colony's progress," she said. "I want to know what's happening there."

Miss Penn paused a moment, as if considering what to say next. Then she drew in a slight breath and continued. "That is why I asked you here today. As the daughter of a book merchant, you will meet people throughout Philadelphia. The colonists love to read—and to discuss what they've read. They will flock to your father's shop, I'm sure. From these patrons you'll learn a great deal about what is happening in the colony.

"I want you to send me reports of the settlement's progress and of its people so I can keep an account of my father's dream. I hope you'll especially note the activities of one man who's causing quite a stir—a Mr. Benjamin Franklin. Since he first arrived in the settlement more than ten years ago, I understand he's encouraged many changes. I want to know what other schemes and ideas he has in mind."

It took all of Suzanna's self-control not to burst out in excitement. This fine lady was asking Suzanna for help, even though she was only fourteen years old! Well, she'd be fifteen by the time she reached the colonies next spring.

As if reading her thoughts, Miss Penn said, "You are young, but I have heard you are not a giggly child and that you have a good mind and clean writing. Put these to work for me, and I will pay you a pound a year."

Suzanna scooted forward in her seat. "Am I to be a spy, then?" she asked.

"No, my dear, there is no need. I did not select you by chance. Your father loves books, and you share that love. Through the books you've read, you've acquired more knowledge than most girls your age, and you've learned to think. Few women in the world today have these advantages. In most of the colonies women are not allowed to attend college, own property, hold a government office, or vote. Believe me when I tell you, many people who come into your father's shop will talk to each other around you as if you weren't there—or as if you hadn't a brain in your head. And even if you told them of your reports to me, most would assume they contained little more than fashion styles and social gossip.

"Simply be who you are—a thoughtful, well-brought-up young lady. You need only show kindness and listen well to gain all the information you need. Will you accept the job?"

Putting her teacup on the tray, Suzanna tried not to look too eager. She would be an investigator and a writer! She took a deep breath to slow down her words. "I would be pleased to do the job, Miss Penn."

Miss Hannah put out her hand and took Suzanna's. "Then I will eagerly await your first letter."

Chapter One
KITE SAILING

July 8, 1736

Miss Penn, your father's colony is almost as big as all of England—and there are twelve other colonies here in America! Nothing feels crowded or squeezed together like at home. Miles stretch between every settlement and farm. When we arrived in Philadelphia I could hardly believe my eyes. The open land your father marked off is now a bustling village of real streets lined with homes and all kinds of shops—silversmiths, cloth dyers, barbers, saddlers, and tradesmen making everything from collars to combs. Now I understand why my father chose to move to America!

But I do miss our English cobblestones. The unpaved streets in Philadelphia either suck my shoes into a bog of mud or cover them with a blanket of dust. Still, dirty shoes are a small price for our new home. My father's shop is twice the size of the place he rented in London, and customers fill it every day.

You're right about the colonists wanting books. Few were brought across the ocean because they were so heavy to pack into the ships. The people missed reading a good story by the fireside. However, I was surprised to find they did have two newspapers to read. Andrew Bradford publishes the *American Weekly Mercury*, but it is not the most popular paper. The *Pennsylvania Gazette* is, and its printed right next door to my father's book shop.

Miss Penn, the publisher of the *Gazette* is Benjamin Franklin, the man you asked me to watch. I couldn't believe it when I saw his sign outside the shop next to my father's. The very man you want me to keep you informed about is my neighbor. And even more incredible, my father already knows him. They met in London ten years ago!

I found this out when Mr. Franklin stopped by to meet us and see our selection of books. He started talking in a friendly way, and the next thing I heard

was my father's startled voice, saying, "You worked for Watt's printing house in London? Why, I bought their books for years."

After hearing this, I listened a lot more carefully. Mr. Franklin said he was born in Boston and learned the printing trade in his older brother's print shop. When he was still but a lad, Mr. Franklin moved to Philadelphia. Later he went to London for a while, then he returned to Philadelphia. Everywhere he went, he worked as a printer. He learned the trade well, and my father says his printing is of the finest quality. His writings are very popular too. We carry all the editions of his popular *Poor Richard's Almanac* in our shop.

Later I met his wife, Deborah, and their two sons. The Franklins love to have people over for dinner and parties. At one gathering Deborah told us about the first time she saw her husband. "Dirt clung to his clothes, and a stocking hung out of his coat pocket," she said. "He had a loaf of bread under each arm as he munched on a third."

She raised her hand to her throat and shook her head before continuing with a merry smile. "You can imagine my shock later when Paul Bradford's father brought a well-dressed Ben to our home, asking my father to let him board with us! After we got acquainted, Ben told me he looked so shabby that first day I saw him because he'd just run away from a harsh apprenticeship in his brother's print shop in Boston. He'd arrived in our settlement tired, hungry, and missing his trunk!"

Soon after that party, I got a chance to see why folks are always talking about Mr. Franklin's unusual ideas. He'd brought his oldest boy to a nearby pond where I'd come to dangle my feet in the cool water. At first they just swam, but then Mr. Franklin got out of the water and started flying a big kite.

The next thing I knew, he told his son, "William, float on your back and hold on to the kite string. The wind will pull you across the water."

It did! William laughed the whole way across as ripples trailed behind him. It looked like so much fun! Then I wondered, *How did Mr. Franklin ever think of such a thing?*

I asked him, and he said, "I was about William's age when I got to thinking about how sails catch the wind and move a boat through water. I supposed a kite could do the same thing, so I tried it. Another time I made paddles for my hands to help me swim faster."

I tell you, Miss Hannah: Benjamin Franklin is an uncommon person. As you said, his ideas are forever creating a stir, especially among the city leaders and Quakers. They'll pass his *Gazette* office then come into our shop and start in. "If that man's not suggesting paper money, then he's starting a library or petitioning to get the streets lighted," they say. "He just cannot leave well-enough alone."

One day a couple of them were here, shaking their heads over Mr. Franklin's latest ideas. Then one of them got a stern look and said, "They need to disband that Leather Apron Club!"

After hearing them speak about the club and its ideas, I asked my father about it. "It is an intellectual club, Suzanna. They call it the *Junto*, which means a joining together of people for a purpose. Mr. Franklin started it a few years ago. The shoemaker and a number of other tradesmen who come to our shop are members. They want to learn as much as possible and share what they learn. They even started a library for loaning out books."

My father says change doesn't come easily, but he believes the *Junto* will eventually bring benefits. I don't know, though. A couple of city officials came into the shop today and said, "Sooner or later the Penns will grow tired of Mr. Franklin and his ideas. Then we'll see whether he and that club of his keep sticking their noses into settlement business!"

Chapter Two
THE BUCKET BRIGADE

February 20, 1739

ire!" How we dread hearing that cry. A small ember glows from a dropped coal or a spark flies out of a fireplace, and the next thing we know flames leap from building to building. Fires have turned parts of our town into piles of black, smoking rubble.

Philadelphia survives fire better than most other communities because many people made their homes and shops out of bricks. But we still lose a lot of buildings, especially in the harbor area where warehouses and homes are built of lumber. Thank goodness Mr. Franklin organized the Union Fire Company, even if he did it with a little trickery.

It all started when we read a letter addressed to Mr. Franklin in the *Gazette*. The "writer" said he was too old to get out and fight fires but wanted to offer a helpful suggestion. He'd seen an organized firefighting group in Boston, and he thought Philadelphia should organize one. He told exactly how to do it. Something

about the writing bothered me. It seemed familiar, yet I didn't know the old man whose signature appeared at the bottom of the letter. Then I saw the last line. "An ounce of prevention is worth a pound of cure."

That's when I knew the writer's real identity. I've read enough issues of *Poor Richard's Almanac* to know Mr. Franklin's writing. The "old man" was really our thirty-three-year-old neighbor who goes on fire calls and keeps healthy by swimming every day!

This isn't the first time he's mixed a little fiction with his facts. Supposedly a Richard Saunders writes *Poor Richard's Almanac*, but everyone knows Mr. Franklin really does it. Somehow his storytelling grabs people's attention better than just writing facts. Take the "old man's" letter, for example. It got the fire company started.

Members of the Junto volunteered first. Soon others joined too. They keep a collection of leather buckets in good order, attend monthly meetings,

and go out on fire calls. As members of the fire brigade they don't have to pay taxes, but if they miss a meeting or fire, they must pay fines. These collected fines allow them to buy more equipment. Though smoke and flames bellowing into the sky still cause a stab of fear, everyone in town feels safer knowing the Union Fire Company is on duty.

A few people still find the Junto's calls for change an irritating pebble in their shoes, but more and more now respect the club. I do! My father let me read the statements that each member must swear to before joining. They show a heart much like your father's, so I copied them for you.

1. That they love mankind, no matter their profession or religion. 2. That they believe no person should be harmed because of opinion or worship. 3. That they love truth, will seek to find it, and tell it to others. 4. That they have no disrespect for any member of the Junto.

When the club meets, members ask each other what they've learned since their last gathering. From what I've overheard in the book shop, the group has talked about Jonathan Swift's essays, uses for South American rubber, and library improvement, among other topics. Mr. Franklin discusses his ideas in the meetings. If the members like a plan, he publishes it in his *Gazette*, suggesting the settlement try it.

Speaking of the library, it is growing quickly. News of it has spread to places you'd never expect. Just last year a doctor in the West Indies sent a thousand dollars to help buy more books! Your brothers also helped by giving the library a plot of land. The Junto wants to build on it because right now all the books are in the home of one of its members. Just think! Our town now has a fire company, and soon it will have its own library building!

Though our settlement makes progress, it also suffers setbacks. Sometimes sickness runs through it like a tidal wave, hitting the young and old, the wealthy and poor. Malaria (some call it the "yellow ghost"), typhoid, and smallpox often kill dozens of people before the epidemic finally goes away.

Trying to find an answer to at least one of these terrible illnesses, a doctor in the city tried a new idea that has been discussed around the colonies who survives smallpox is unlikely to get the disease again, so the doctor *inoculated* fifty people with smallpox. He hoped, as others have said, that the tiny dose would cause only a slight sickness while still creating what the body needs to fight the disease. Mr. Franklin spoke highly of the results. "All recovered except a child of the doctor's, who is thought to have been infected earlier."

In spite of these words, Mr. Franklin did not get his own young sons, William and Francis, inoculated. Perhaps the death of the doctor's child made him hold off. Whatever the reason, Francis caught the awful sickness and died. He was only four years old.

For a while after little Francis's death, the *Gazette* printed no ideas for change. It stuck to the news. Then Mr. Franklin heard the rumor that parents were refusing to get their children inoculated because they thought Francis had died after having the treatment. Despite his grief, our neighbor wrote to stop this dangerous untruth. "Though I publicly supported the treatment, I did not get it for my son," he said.

I could almost see teardrops on the paper as I read it.

Much later, Mr. Franklin's old interests returned. Again the Junto and the *Gazette* promoted change. Then something happened. I wish I did not have to tell you about it, Miss Hannah, but it concerns your father's "holy experiment," so I must.

Your brothers and Mr. Franklin are at odds. After listening to my father and others talk, I believe I understand what happened. When your father purchased land from the Delaware Indians, he was given an option to buy more—as much as a person could walk in a day and a half. Recently this tribe had trouble with the Iroquois. Your brothers offered to protect the Delawares from the Iroquois if the Delawares would allow the "walking purchase."

When the Indians agreed, your brothers hired three of the hardiest woodsmen in the colony. Instead of walking heel-to-toe, as the Indians thought they would do, the woodsmen took off at a pace that exhausted the Delawares who went with them. Continuing on after the Indians fell behind, the men even ran. By the end of the day and a half, they had covered sixty-five miles—far more than the Delawares expected.

Since Mr. Franklin is now the clerk in the Pennsylvania Assembly, he heard about the affair firsthand. Immediately he went to your brothers' home. A servant told me what happened. "Mr. Franklin didn't yell, but he looked nigh on to bursting his buttons. He said, 'You cheated the Delawares, and they won't forget it. By risking the good relationship your father established with the Indians, you have endangered us all!'"

Miss Hannah, I must side with Mr. Franklin. I have the utmost respect for you and your father, but the "walking purchase" does not hold with his dreams for this colony. Though I am sad to take exception to your brothers' behavior, I cannot pretend to approve of it. Because of this, I will understand if you do not wish to hear from me again.

Chapter Three
MAGIC SQUARES AND MAIL

November 23, 1743

It relieved me to get your letter, asking that I keep sending my reports. I enjoy listening, learning, and writing things down. But I am not the only one. Mr. Franklin does too. It amazes me that he continues to learn, even though he's a successful businessman. He studies books twelve hours a week! And he's even taught himself how to speak French, Italian, Spanish, and Latin!

It's hard to believe he only attended school for two years before starting work in his family's candlemaking shop when he was ten years old. He once told my father, "I hated dipping wax all day. My parents knew it and feared I'd run off to sea like an older brother had done. So they took me around to visit shops that offered apprenticeships. My liking for reading and writing drew me to printing."

Though our neighbor had little schooling, that will not be true of the children in Philadelphia. Its settlers believe in education. Right after your father landed, the town hired a scholar to teach reading, writing, and arithmetic. A few years later, the Quakers started a school for black children.

Though some Pennsylvanians own slaves, many are opposed to slavery. In the other colonies, people think nothing of owning other human beings, but here, the Quaker influence makes it frowned upon. Mr. Franklin is even talking of starting a group to abolish slavery.

Another strong religious influence recently came to our colony, a preacher by the name of George Whitefield. His passion for God and his thrilling voice drew thousands to listen to him. Even Mr. Franklin became this preacher's friend. At first our neighbor worried about Mr. Whitefield's popularity because he never again wants to see rulers force one religion on people. But I've heard these two men talk of God, government, love, and their fellow man. They agree on many of these issues, and I think this led them to start an alms house and charity school for the poor and orphaned. But even with this joint project, their friendship can only be called unique.

Why, one time I saw Mr. Franklin walking backward from one of Mr. Whitefield's street preachings. When I got closer, I heard him counting. After going a few blocks, he stopped and did some figures. Finally, I had to ask what he was doing.

He answered, "I've always doubted those newspaper accounts of Whitefield preaching to twenty-five thousand people. It didn't seem reasonable that a voice could carry that far, but I just marked off the distance that I could hear him. Then I figured how many people could fit in a circle of that size around him. It put my doubts to rest. According to my figures, thirty thousand people could hear this man preach!"

When I told my father about it, he just shook his head and said, "Did you know Mr. Franklin did poorly in math in school?"

I couldn't believe it! Men in the Assembly come into our shop all the time and talk about Franklin's amazing "magic squares." He draws them on paper, dividing them into equal sections and putting numbers in each one. The last square he showed me had sixteen sections, and no matter how you added up the rows, horizontally, vertically, or diagonally, they always totaled 260!"

It's hard to imagine Mr. Franklin doing poorly in anything. In addition to being the Assembly clerk, he also is our postmaster. Before he took control, the letters that came from England ended up in a public coffeehouse, where they waited until someone claimed them. The letters carried by the postriders between Boston and Philadelphia also landed there. Letters from the rest of the colonies, brought by travelers who agreed to carry them, were added to the pile.

However, since Mr. Franklin became postmaster, things are much better. When a letter arrives by ship, postrider, or traveler, he takes care of it and advertises in the newspaper for the addressee to pick it up. Though it still takes many months for your letters to reach me, at least I now know when they arrive in town.

Letters aren't the only thing arriving in your father's settlement of "brotherly love." People from Europe scramble down the ramps of every ship that docks in our harbor. Amish, Mennonites, Lutherans, and others come, seeking the freedom to worship as they please. But more than the religious seek a new life in our colony. Immigrants from troubled countries such as Germany, Ireland, and Scotland also

pour out of the ships. Six thousand new people arrived just this year. When you think that nearly thirty-five thousand people now live here, it doesn't take magic squares to realize your father's settlement is turning into a big town. Our streets get longer and longer as more homes and shops are built.

As the town grows, so do Mr. Franklin's new ideas and changes. His latest notion is a scientific group called the *American Philosophical Society*. To get it started, he wrote to his friends in our colony as well as in New Jersey, Delaware, New York, and New England. He suggested that they share information about plants, minerals, diseases, fossils, chemicals, inventions, maps, and so many other things I cannot name them all.

This society isn't causing the fuss that the Junto first did. I think Philadelphia is getting used to Benjamin Franklin. But I think its citizens would be wise not to get too comfortable. Knowing my neighbor, he could still have a jolt or two in store for us!

Chapter Four
A LAUGH AND A KISS

April 2, 1747

When I worried about Mr. Franklin still having a jolt or two in store for Philadelphia, I thought it would be a new idea or an invention—not a real jolt that would make us laugh. But I should have known better.

Ever since moving here, my father and I have laughed at the clever things that appear in *Poor Richard's Almanac*. Our neighbor's clever mix of facts with fiction often leaves us wondering if he's pulling our leg or spying in our window, discovering all the half-witted things we do each day.

For months I thought Richard Saunders, the "writer" of the almanac's first page, was a real person. Everyone in town knows somebody just like the fellow—a poor, uneducated farmer with good horse sense. We even read about his fine wife, Bridget, and feel as if we know her too. The couple's troubles and triumphs sound like many of the things all families go through. No wonder they seem so real!

But when I found myself laughing at so many silly astrology predictions and exaggerations, I realized only Mr. Franklin's humor and creativity could have produced this entertaining couple. Even a lot of their "horse sense" wisdom makes folks smile. Here are some samples: "Three may keep a secret, if two of them are dead." "He that lieth down with dogs shall rise up with fleas." "Fish and visitors stink in three days."

No wonder *Poor Richard's Almanac* is such a big seller in the colonies—ten thousand copies every year!

I talked with Mr. Franklin about his writing, and he let me read some of his early work. My favorite is about hoop petticoats. He wrote it years ago under the pen name Silence Dogood. It says, "These monstrous topsy-turvy pieces are not fit for the church, the hall, or the kitchen. If a number of them were mounted in Boston's harbor, they would look more

like engines of war for bombing the town than ornaments of the fair sex."

As I laughed at his comments about our mode of dress, it came to me that I should write about the men's fashion of wearing wigs. All males wear them—boys, servants, Quakers, and even the poor men. They are made of stiff horsehair and look nothing like the real thing. And what styles! Just read their names: bobs, majors, spencers, foxtails, twist, scratches, and many more. They might not look like war engines, but more than one man has had the "wool pulled over his eyes" by rascals who yank on the wig and pull it lopsided. Their intention is

usually to poke fun at the man—or to blind him so he can be robbed. Oh, to see them pulled off! They are hideous!

I fear I'm getting carried away and best return to Mr. Franklin's jolt. Last year he heard a lecture on a new discovery called *electricity*. Later our library received a glass tube as a gift. An electrical charge is created when you drag a silk scarf through the tube. Mr. Franklin and his friends have spent hours testing it and other gadgets like it. Now he entertains people at his parties with electricity. He uses it to relight candles that have been blown out. He also makes lightning arcs by passing a charged wire over a painted plate, and he even gets a cork-and-thread "spider" to dance on tabletops.

But everyone's favorite is the electric kiss. Mr. Franklin tells a girl to stand on a wax pad and hold the charged glass tube. Then he gets a lad, who, like the girl, takes hold of a wire connected to the tube. When their lips get close, a shocking electrical jolt flies between them!

Besides enjoying his electrical fun, we always sing and dance at the Franklin parties. Recently a man who just came from France showed us a new dance called the cotillion. Couples move together, making fancy patterns with their steps. At first we laughed more than we danced because everyone kept making mistakes. But once we got the patterns figured out, we went round and round the room.

Having music is never a problem when our neighbor is around. He plays so many instruments. I struggle just to master the piano while he does well on the guitar, harp, and violin. He's even working on making his own instrument of glass!

Speaking of music, a newly arrived immigrant from England came to our shop, wanting to sell a couple of books. My father asked him many questions about our old country. At first he told us of the new complicated game called cricket that is growing in popularity in England. But then he spoke about my father's favorite opera composer, George Handel. The immigrant told us, "Handel's latest work is quite successful. It is called the *Messiah*. People especially like the part called the 'Hallelujah Chorus.'"

I don't know if we'll ever get to hear it, but the first play to be performed in the city was presented not long ago. And our shop recently got a book by an unusual writer—a black woman named Terry Lucy Prince, who has written a poem about an Indian attack. Miss Lucy was kidnapped from Africa and sold into colonial slavery as a child. No one knows how she learned to read and write, especially since she is only sixteen years old! I believe the colonies will produce many fine writers one day.

Reading back over this report, I see my news has not been very serious. Perhaps I've shared these light-hearted notes out of fear that I'll have little such news in the days ahead. With France and Spain at war again with England, the news around us grows darker each day. The French attack the colonies from the North, and the Spanish attack from the South. So far, we've heard no cannons boom or muskets fire—but how long will this quiet continue? Our small harbor is now an important port, and much shipping comes in and out of it. Both the French and the Spanish would love to control it.

Chapter Five
MAN THE WALLS!

January 1, 1748

Every other colony builds defenses, yet our land, beaches, and riverways remain undefended. A well-armed privateer could easily enter our harbor and take us as a prize of war. No cannons or militia would stop the ship or its pirate crew."

Mr. Franklin's words made me shudder—especially the word "privateer"! At least officers commanded the French and Spanish sailors, but the privateers obey only their greed and lust. Though men don't talk of such things in front of women, we still hear of the vicious burning and looting done by these cruel sailors.

Even before Mr. Franklin spoke of our needing defense, Anna Penrose had spoken to me about it. She runs her family's shipbuilding business and often goes to the harbor.

"Make no mistake," she said. "France or Spain would gladly capture Philadelphia. Our rich mines produce lots of iron. And a shipload of our wheat, flour, cattle, and sheep brings a fifty-thousand-pound profit. In addition, we build the finest ships in the colonies. It is only a matter of time before the war reaches us."

After hearing Anna's description of our danger, I welcomed Mr. Franklin's call for defense. But the Quakers did not. They don't believe in fighting, and our neighbor's constant urging for a militia, forts, lighthouses, and other defenses created a battle about battles! In the end, Mr. Franklin and his supporters won, but not in the way you might have expected them to.

He didn't use harsh words and verbal fights. Instead he turned to his printing press and created a pamphlet called *Plain Truth*. It exposed Philadelphia's danger and offered logical arguments for defending the city. He didn't dismiss the Quakers' faith but instead quoted the Bible to show defensive war wasn't wrong. Then he went before our Quaker-held Assembly and told about members of their faith who had defended themselves.

He never asked the Quakers to violate their beliefs by approving money for war. Instead he asked for money "for the king's use." Mr. Franklin's knack of avoiding trouble with the Quakers by using clever wording almost caused my eavesdropping to be revealed one day. Two Assembly members came into the shop and were talking about the latest vote that approved money for our new militia. "I never thought Ben could get the Quakers to approve buying gunpowder. Then I saw how he worded the request: 'for the purchase of bread, flour, wheat, and other grains.'"

It took a moment before I realized the "other grains" were grains of gunpowder!

I just had to laugh, but if I did, the men would realize I was listening to them. So I dashed out the door and turned up the street, giggling my way past the other shops. No wonder my father says Mr. Franklin would make a good diplomat!

Whoops, I must finish my news. I need to explain about getting our new militia.

A few days after *Plain Truth* was published, Mr. Franklin called a town meeting. My father went and later told me, "Our neighbor repeated the arguments in his pamphlet and then called on the colonists to join an Association for Defense. Though I share the Quakers' passion for peace, I joined. I cannot stand by and leave my family unprotected."

Twelve hundred men joined the Association for Defense that night, and within days the group grew to ten thousand. Right now nearly every man who isn't a Quaker has joined, bought a weapon, and practices defense drills. Mr. Franklin even carries a musket among the soldiers. In addition to those guarding our city, regiments were formed to help the colonies north of us who are being attacked. Many of the women, myself included, made silk colors for the regiments to wear. These will identify our men as part of our regiment from Pennsylvania.

Mr. Franklin did not stop with forming a militia. We now have cannons behind a log-and-earth wall protecting our most exposed border. Once again, our clever neighbor achieved what others could never have done. He got the cannons. A few old ones came from Boston, but our eighteen new ones came from the governor of New York—though I suspect he regrets it now that his head is clear.

I heard the story of the new cannons when Mr. Franklin told it to my father. "Five of us went to Governor Clinton and asked for cannons," he said. "Right away the governor said no, but he did ask us to dine with him and his counsel. I'm afraid their

dinner custom included a great deal of Madeira wine. As the evening went on, the governor very good-naturedly changed his mind. First he gave us six cannons, then ten, and finally eighteen!"

It pleased me to hear Mr. Franklin laugh with my father. I'm afraid he hasn't had much to smile about lately. Many say that his stand for defense will hurt his good relations with the Quakers in the Assembly. I even heard one man in our shop say, "I've always wanted to be the Assembly clerk. I think I'll suggest to Benjamin that he needs to resign."

The man did suggest it, but Mr. Franklin looked right into his eyes and said, "I shall never ask, never refuse, and never resign an office."

Even though there's been talk about our neighbor, all of us, including most of the Quakers, sleep much better knowing that privateers and soldiers can't just march into our town. Everyone knows we are no longer a small settlement with little to lose. Philadelphia needed defenses on its growing borders.

Because the governor, council members, and town leaders recognize this need, they still speak highly of Mr. Franklin when they come into our shop, and I don't fear for his standing in our community. However, I do worry about his attraction to electricity. I live in dread that one day I'll enter his shop next door and find him shocked insensible.

Chapter Six
TURKEY SHOCK

December 24, 1750

My worst fear came true, but it didn't happen in Mr. Franklin's printing shop. It happened when he tried to kill a Christmas turkey!

Everything about electricity fascinates our neighbor. When he only had the glass tube that made shocking kisses, nothing got out of hand. But a few years ago he heard about something better. It's a jar covered with metal sheets inside and out, filled with water, and plugged with a cork stopper. A wire extends through the cork and into the water. This "Leyden jar," as it is called, *stores* electricity and can give off a much more powerful shock than the glass tube did.

Mr. Franklin did many experiments with the Leyden jar, trying to find out how it held power.

He was forever talking of *positive* and *negative* *charges*. Finally he came up with a jar that he called an *electrical battery*. Its powerful shock can even burn things! Well, watching the battery work one day, our neighbor decided he could kill his Christmas turkey by shocking it to death. In truth, he came nearer to shocking himself to death!

His wife was in such a panic over the whole thing she blurted out the story to me. "Ben made two extra-large jar batteries. He said they had the power of forty regular ones and would surely kill a turkey. He was holding on to a chain that connected the two jars when all of a sudden a bright light flashed and a sound like a pistol fired! Ben started shaking violently. He said he lost consciousness for only a few seconds, but he was sore and numb until the next morning. Needless to say, our turkey ended up getting the ax!"

Though Mr. Franklin's work with electricity is unnerving at times, many of his other interests prove quite helpful. He watches nature very carefully and sees things no one else notices. One such discovery kept us much warmer this winter.

It all started when he saw that air moved differently, depending on if it was hot or cold. After studying it for a while, he thought the information might improve our smoky chimneys and reduce the amount of wood we burned in our fireplaces. Next thing I hear he's at one of the settlement's foundries, having an *iron* fireplace cast. Then he printed a pamphlet, explaining how to use his "Franklin stove," as he calls it, to warm a house.

The stove pleased the governor so much he offered to give Mr. Franklin a patent on the invention. Our neighbor told him, "Oh no. We enjoy advantages from the inventions of others, and I am glad to serve people without thought of profit."

Another useful discovery that Mr. Franklin made had to do with colors. He told my father the whole thing started when he tried to set paper on fire with a magnifying glass. He noticed that white paper did not burn easily. But if he focused the glass's light beam on a black dot or a letter, it burst into flame much more quickly. That set him to wondering about colors and heat. What he did next was truly odd.

Walking to the shop on a sunny winter day, I saw my neighbor laying pieces of cloth on the snow. It looked like a giant patchwork quilt made of every color you could think of: black, deep blue, a lighter blue, green, purple, red, yellow, white, and more. Finally I asked, "What on earth are you doing?"

"I'm proving a theory," he said confidently. "I believe dark colors hold heat. If it's true, then the snow under the dark fabrics should melt faster than the snow under the light-colored ones."

He was right! An hour later, the black square had sunk deep into the snow. The lighter the color, the less each square had sunk, and the white one sat on unmelted snow. Excited by his discovery, Mr. Franklin started talking more to himself than to me. "This means soldiers in deserts should wear light-colored uniforms," he said, "and those in cold need dark ones."

Not everything Mr. Franklin discovers turns out to be useful, but most Philadelphians agree his ideas are always interesting. I especially liked it when he proved that ants could talk to each other. He did this by taking some syrup and putting it in a clay jar. He hung the jar from a closet ceiling by a piece of string. Then he put one single ant in the jar. The ant ate the syrup until it was apparently full. Then it struggled to get out of the pot, finally finding its way up the string and onto the ceiling. It scurried around a while, then managed to find its way back to the ant colony. Within half an hour, a whole army of ants was marching up the wall, across the ceiling, and down the string!

Other people in the colonies share Mr. Franklin's interest in nature. A woman from South Carolina stopped in our book shop, looking for journals on indigo. Her name was Eliza Pinckney, and as I helped her, she said, "Plants have fascinated me since before I started running my father's plantations as a young girl. So when I saw we needed a cash crop and the fabric industry needed a blue dye, I went to work. I bred and crossbred indigo plants until they produced lots of seeds containing a clear blue dye."

Later I took tea with Anna Penrose and told her about my new friend. "Well, I'll be!" Anna said as she stopped in the middle of sipping her tea and put down her cup. "So *that's* why South Carolina's shipping turned around. People said it was because the war with France and Spain ended, but I knew it had to be more. Just a few years ago, the colony only exported 5,000 pounds of indigo. Last year, it shipped out 130,000 pounds!"

As the colonies have prospered, so has Mr. Franklin. His publishing has made him a wealthy man, at least by colony standards. He speaks of retiring to a leisure of books and good conversation. Another man now runs his publishing office for him, and he has stopped writing *Poor Richard's Almanac*. I can't help wondering if this means Mr. Franklin will no longer shake up your father's city with ideas of change and improvement. I pray not!

Though our town's iron foundries and shipbuilding grow, without news of my neighbor's activities, my reports will be quite dull.

Chapter Seven
A FLASH OF LIGHTNING

September 12, 1752

It's a disaster, and no one knows exactly what to do. It all started last year when the town leaders voted to put a bell in the steeple of our new statehouse. But they didn't want just any bell—they wanted the biggest one in all the colonies!

The *Gazette* printed an article that told us the details. It read, "Our city leaders recently wrote to the best bell-makers in England, asking them to forge a two-thousand-pound bell from the finest materials. Inscribed on its side will be the Bible verse found in Leviticus 25:10: *'Proclaim liberty throughout all the land to all the inhabitants thereof.'*"

When the bell arrived this summer, everyone wanted to see it. The wagon carrying it rumbled and creaked from the harbor to the statehouse, and people lined the streets, just like for a parade. I peeked around a woman's bonnet and caught sight of the huge bell. The man beside me put my amazement into words. "Thunder and tarnation! Would you look at the size of it!"

Another person said, "We will be the envy of all the colonies. None of them have such a handsome and mighty bell."

No one wanted to wait to hear it ring. So instead of mounting it in the steeple, workmen built a frame on the statehouse lawn and hung the bell there. The whole town cheered as it rang out once, twice—and then the disaster struck!

When the clapper hit the bell's insides a third time, it only thudded. The cheers turned into gasps. I held my breath as I watched the bell ringer cling to the rope, trying to still it. The town leaders rushed to inspect it. "Look! It's cracked!" a man yelled.

Though no one knew what to do for sure, the owner of one of our iron foundries volunteered to break up the bell, melt it down, and recast it. Yesterday I heard an Assemblyman tell my father that copper was going to be added to strengthen it. We all hope to hear it ring again soon.

Speaking of Assemblymen, Mr. Franklin is now one. His retirement is hardly a relaxed life. Recently he told my father, "The public, now considering me a man of leisure, calls me for their purposes, giving me duties in almost every part of our civil government."

I'm afraid it's true. Besides the Assembly, many other jobs demand his time. He continues to build our colony's defenses, since France and Spain would still like to claim more of the Americas. He also has worked on keeping us safe from ourselves.

For years Mr. Franklin wrote articles opposing our constable system because it often caused more harm than safety. Whoever's turn it was to police an area could pay the local constable to get out of the duty. The money should have been used to hire replacements, but most of the time it jangled in the constable's pocket, buying strong drink and cheap rascals who neglected to walk the rounds. As a result, few people liked to be out at night.

But thanks to Mr. Franklin's reforms, the town hires men to police areas, paying them from a special tax on property. We also have lighted streets. Our neighbor designed a practical square-shaped lamp with flat panes of glass that can be easily cleaned and replaced. Each day at dusk, a man goes around lighting the candles in them. Why, at this rate Philadelphia will soon look as grand as London!

In spite of all his jobs in the colony, nothing sidetracks Mr. Franklin's interest in electricity. His experiments have uncovered so much about this new power that the British Royal Society honored him with their Copley Medal of Science.

It was my good fortune to see one of his greatest experiments.

For months I'd heard Mr. Franklin tell my father and members of the Junto, "The electricity made with our batteries is similar to lightning. I suspect lightning bolts are actually electrical fire."

A few weeks later I heard that a Frenchman had proved Mr. Franklin's theory. I couldn't imagine how until I went out in a storm, trying to find my cat, Gulliver. By the time I discovered him outside a barn, I was soaked. I turned to rush home but stopped when I saw a kite flying among the raindrops and lightning bolts. A key was dangling from the kite, and the string looped downward, disappearing into the barn's door.

In spite of the downpour, I had to know who would be playing with a kite in such weather. With Gulliver meowing in my arms, I hurried into the barn, ready to scold a child for being out in such a

dreadful storm. Imagine my shock when I found Mr. Franklin and his son at the end of the kite string! Then another shock hit. I mean a real shock: Lightning! The charge hit a metal rod attached to the kite, ran down the silk string and entered the key. Mr. Franklin touched his knuckle to the key and got a shock. Lightning *is* electricity, but you'll NEVER catch me doing this experiment!

But simply proving something has never been enough for Mr. Franklin. He always wants to find a practical use for it. That's when he came up with the lightning rod idea. He says if you put a metal bar on a house or barn, extending it from the rooftop into the ground, when lightning strikes it, the charge will be diverted into the ground instead of damaging the building.

But I fear that lightning is the least of our worries right now. The French are once again moving against the colonies, and soldiers are fighting in the North. But an even bigger concern is the Indians. The French stir them up, making the Indians angry at the settlers in our colony—which isn't hard since the tribes have not forgotten the deceitful "walking purchase."

Chapter Eight
COLONEL AND DIPLOMAT

October 8, 1755

We're at war with the French and the Indians. Your brother John, Mr. Franklin, and some others went to a defense-planning conference called by the king. Representatives from seven colonies came. When it ended, Mr. Franklin returned to his printing press.

In the *Gazette* he wrote that we cannot hope to win against the French unless the colonies unite. Next to his writing, he drew a picture—a rattlesnake cut in pieces. He put a colony's name on each piece and wrote beneath the disjointed snake, "Join or die."

Even though Mr. Franklin's waistline is noticeably thicker now and I worry about his health, he is not limiting his role to just meetings and writings. He is now a colonel in our militia, and he supervised the building of forts along our northwest boundary.

Even so, I feared the worst when a wagon full of wounded British soldiers came into town. As we helped care for them, I heard a soldier tell what happened.

"Commander Edward Braddock of His Majesty's forces planned to attack a French fort just beyond your border. But the French, with their Indian allies, ambushed our troops, killing most of our men. George Washington pulled us survivors together and led us to safety. He then ordered the wounded to be taken to the nearest town that had a doctor."

Everyone knew our colony would be attacked next. As the raids got closer to Philadelphia, my fears got bigger! I knew the Quakers wouldn't fight. Could our militia save the city?

About that time, Mr. Franklin mounted his horse and led our militia against the French. They did what Braddock could not—defeated the enemy. We rang our new bell to celebrate. That's right, our two-thousand-pound bell is now hanging in our statehouse and doing its job. It took a couple of tries, but our blacksmiths finally repaired it.

As the fighting moved to other colonies, Mr. Franklin went back to improving our city. We now have a hospital. One of his doctor friends suggested it for taking care of sick immigrants. However, no other colony had one, so he couldn't raise enough money to build it. That's when our neighbor got involved.

Right away he wrote an article in the *Gazette,* calling for the town's support. Some money came in but not enough. Then he asked the Assembly to match what the community gave. That did it. When Philadelphians heard that each of their dollars would be matched with another one from the government, enough money came in. Mr. Franklin wrote the message that's carved into the base of the building: *Founded for the relief of the sick and miserable. May the God of mercies bless the undertaking.*

Our neighbor thrives on new undertakings! This year he started "Hand-in-Hand." It is the first insurance company in the colonies. People who pay to join will get money to rebuild their houses if fires burn them down.

You can tell an insured home because it has a metal disk on it, showing two clasped hands. However, a house can't be insured if a tree stands near it. Also, the company directors don't get paid. Instead, every year they get a dinner of pickled oysters and gingersnaps shaped like S's.

Mr. Franklin also started a university in town, and he's its president!

With all this "retirement" activity, I was afraid Mr. Franklin would lose his sense of humor. However, he recently put my fears to rest. He had been telling the local farmers that plaster of Paris made a good fertilizer. They wouldn't listen and continued in their old ways. So one day he went into a field and sprinkled the white powder in large letters that read, "THIS HAS BEEN PLASTERED."

At first the farmer was upset, but soon his anger turned to laughter as everyone joked about the ridiculous message. When the letters disappeared into the soil, the event was forgotten—until spring. Then the letters reappeared, but this time in rich, thick, emerald-green grass. The pale, sparse grass surrounding the letters left little doubt about the quality of the fertilizer. I suspect all the farmers will "plaster" their fields next year!

Though much of my news includes Ben Franklin, we've also heard much talk of George Washington and other men like John Hancock and Samuel Adams. These men are making a name for themselves in the colonies. I am glad, because I think we will see very little of Mr. Franklin in the years ahead. My father's prediction about our neighbor making a good diplomat is coming true.

Philadelphia is now one of the largest cities in the colonies. With its change from a settlement to an important city, government problems often affect us. The Pennsylvania Assembly and the Pennsylvania governor are at odds about providing money to defend our outlying settlements. After the governor refused to support a single bill that would help these unprotected people, he took off for England to tell the king about his problems. That's when the Assembly voted to send Mr. Franklin to England also, to represent *them* before the king.

He sails soon, leaving behind his wife and friends. His son William will go with him. Soon you will be able to get news of the colonies directly from Mr. Franklin, so you no longer need to pay me for reports. I will miss being your eyes and ears in Pennsylvania, but I plan to keep a diary for myself. I've enjoyed writing for these many years, though it will probably be quite dull without my neighbor's wit and ideas to stir the people.

Even without him here, I will not be able to forget Mr. Franklin. Everywhere I look in the city, reminders of him surround me—the library, the hospital, the insurance company, the post office. Even the streetlights, fire pumpers, and night-watch boxes will bring to mind this great citizen and friend. Because of him, your father's plans for a fine settlement have prospered, and now Philadelphia is a big and important city. And because of him, your father's dream for a free and prospering colony is a reality.

Epilogue
DEAR DIARY

July 4, 1776

Many years have passed since I sat in Miss Hannah Penn's parlor. Wrinkles and gray hair now hide the young girl who sat so straight, pretending a book balanced on her head. But in spite of the years, I must write again of William Penn and his colony.

This fine man's ideals of accepting all people and allowing them to govern themselves are more real now than when I wrote of them in my last report to his daughter. Back then, we were protecting our colonies from the French. Today we declared our independence from England.

As anyone who knows him could have guessed, Mr. Franklin is in the thick of our struggle. He has more waistline and less hair, but age still doesn't hold him back. In England he struggled for years to build a strong British-American union. He constantly sent letters to their newspapers, arguing the need to end the unfair taxes and laws ordered by King George. He also urged the patriots back in the colonies to compromise a little.

But in the end, English officials accused him of starting the American rebellion and fired him from his job as the colonies' postmaster. Then they tried to bribe him. If he got the colonists to behave, they said, he would be appointed to another position. Tired and fed up, he told them, "To join America to such a corrupt Britain would be like joining together the dead and the living."

On returning to Pennsylvania, he attended the First and Second Continental Congress and helped Thomas Jefferson write our Declaration of Independence. Now the fighting has begun, and George Washington, the militia colonel from the French and Indian War, is the commander in chief of our troops.

As in the past, Mr. Franklin is not limited by war. He still thinks of ideas like most men think of food.

Why, even the eyeglasses sitting on the end of his nose came from one of his brainstorms. He calls them *bifocals*. The upper half of the lens allows him to see far away while the lower half helps him see up close!

Besides continuing to invent things, nature still holds Mr. Franklin's attention. He's written of ocean water, sunspots, shooting stars, rainfall, whirlwinds, and earthquakes. I believe that one day he will receive praise as a great scientist. But even with all this, his interest in the public's improvement hasn't stopped. He has formed a group to stop slavery.

Philadelphia is now the center of our new country's government. But that is not all. Our shipbuilders are making most of the American navy's vessels, building fifty-four ships, including six big frigates with twenty-six to sixty guns. Also, more than fifty iron furnaces and forges in the city are making hundreds of long rifles. In addition, they're turning out cannonballs, wagon-wheel rims, and chains to put across the rivers to hold back the English fleet.

Besides helping the Revolution, our city continues to make other progress. Thanks to another Franklin idea, we now have paved streets. No longer do my shoes either sink in mud or get covered in dust. This is especially nice since we now have many theaters, and traveling to them is no longer the chore it once was. Though George Handel is dead, we can hear his music performed here. We even listen to melodies played on the new instrument Mr. Franklin invented; it's called the glass armonica. It makes shimmering, bell-like sounds when fingers touch the wet glass circles arranged on a spindle.

I fear we will need the pleasure of our theaters in the days ahead. Mr. Franklin is returning to England to seek a treaty of freedom, but I do not think King George will give up his rich colonies easily. The Penns, however, sold their proprietorship for 130,000 pounds instead of fighting to keep it. Though they still own their land, family members no longer affect our government. When we declared our independence, we stopped being a colony and started becoming a free country.

Perhaps Mr. Franklin's prayer for all countries says it best:

"God grant that not only the love of liberty, but a total understanding of the rights of man, may enter all the nations of the earth, so that a thinker may set his foot anywhere on its surface and say, 'This is my country.'"

Service

Character Building with Benjamin Franklin

Service:

Giving Others a Helping Hand

Can you get through one day without help? If you think you can, you're wrong! Without your parents' support, you wouldn't have food to eat or a bed to sleep in. Without a librarian's directions, you wouldn't know how to find a book. Without doctor's aid, you'd struggle to get well. The list of those who help us is endless.

From clerks waiting on us in stores to friends playing on our ball team, people serve us every day. Service, according to the dictionary, means "being of assistance to another." The man you read about Benjamin Franklin, lived a life of service. Whether he was doing scientific experiments, printing his newspaper, or taking part in Philadelphia's government, he was always thinking of ways to help the people in his community.

Like Ben Franklin, we live in a community. People surround us at school, in our neighborhood, and in shopping malls. But unlike Ben, we often think of serving others as hard, boring, time consuming, and bothersome. That's why it is important to take a closer look at this part of Ben's life. Why did he like serving others? What attracted him to it? How come he didn't consider it hard or bothersome?

Answering these questions, along with digging into Bible verses and the quotes of others, should help you understand why Ben Franklin served so many. You'll also discover the value God places on serving one another and why it needs to be a part of how we live.

Kite Sailing

God has so ordered that men,
being in need of each other, should learn to love each other,
and bear each other's burdens.

G . A . S A L A

1. Review chapter one and write down two people Ben Franklin helped and how he "served" them.

_____ : _____

_____ : _____

Remember, service is more than just hard work—more than taking out the trash or mowing the lawn. It can be listening when someone is upset, showing a person how to have fun, or even helping a friend find a book.

2. People can serve at their job, at home, or around their town. Ben Franklin looked for ways to serve no matter where he was. Write down three places that Ben served.

_____

_____

STUCK? *Think about his job, his family, and the ideas he thought of for his town.*

W H A T   T H E   B I B L E   S A Y S

Read Mark 10:45

For even the Son of Man did not come to be served, but to serve,
and to give His life—a ransom for many.

Ben Franklin isn't the only person we have as an example of someone who served others. Who does this verse say came to serve and to die for us?

I T ' S   Y O U R   T U R N

Think about all the things you did today. In the space below, write down specific times that you helped (served) other people. If you can't think of any, pray for opportunities to serve others tomorrow.

The Bucket Brigade

Light is the task when many share the toil.
H O M E R

1. Look back over chapter two and write down two times when people worked together to help others.

_____

_____

_____

Today we have big fire departments, and medicine can cure most illnesses. If you imagine what it would be like not to have these when a fire broke out or a person got sick, you'll easily spot two times people worked together to serve others.

2. We can learn about service by noting the wrong way to deal with other people. Write down a time in chapter two when people did not serve others, but hurt them.

_____

_____

STUCK? *The Native Americans did not look like Ben Franklin and the other white settlers back in 1739. Did that make it OK not to serve but to cheat them?*

WHAT THE BIBLE SAYS

Read 1 Thessalonians 5:11
Therefore encourage one another
and build each other up as you are already doing.

In this verse God is not asking us to do something; He is commanding us to do something. What is His command?

IT'S YOUR TURN

Knowing that God commands us to do something doesn't make it easy. Pray and ask God to help you encourage and serve other people.

Magic Squares and Mail

All work is as seed sown; it grows and spreads, and sows itself anew.
THOMAS CARLYLE

1. Go back over chapter three. Find three kinds of service that Ben Franklin did that you can find in your town today.

_____

_____

_____

When a person serves another, many times people like it so much they do it too. What started as simply hiring a "scholar," sharing with people about God, and getting a letter to its owner turned into big helps that we have today.

2. Why do you think Ben Franklin's service to improve the delivering of mail eventually became the huge postal service that we enjoy today?

_____

_____

STUCK? *Think about all the new people coming from all over the world to Philadelphia.*

WHAT THE BIBLE SAYS

Read 2 Corinthians 9:6
Remember this: the person who sows sparingly
will also reap sparingly,
and the person who sows generously will also reap generously.

God says that giving our time, energy, and money will not be wasted. What promise does He make to us if we do a lot to serve others?

IT'S YOUR TURN

Think about a time when you served or helped a friend, teacher, or parent. Now think about the people who saw you do it. Ask God to use your service as an example to others. That way they might want to serve too!

A Laugh and a Kiss

Little deeds of kindness,
Little words of love,
Help to make earth happy
Like the heaven above.

JULIA FLETCHER CARNEY

1. Service can be done with a smile! Review this chapter and write down two times Ben Franklin took the time to help another person laugh and smile.

_____

_____

_____

In the 1700s people didn't have televisions, video games, or radios. There weren't any football games to go to or malls to visit. Mr. Franklin was pretty smart to think of these different ways to help people be entertained.

2. Name three things that Mr. Franklin used to help brighten the days of others.

_____

_____

STUCK? *We have stereos, toys, and books. What did Mr. Franklin use?*

WHAT THE BIBLE SAYS

Read Colossians 3:23
Whatever you do, do it enthusiastically,
as something done for the Lord and not for men.

This verse talks about working or helping others. It also says God likes smiles, good humor, and laughter. What is the word that tells us this?

IT'S YOUR TURN

Write down some of the things you did today to help or serve others. Put a smiley face by the ones you did with a smile. Put a frowny face by the ones you groaned about. Talk to God about the number of smiles and frowns you had. Ask Him to help you smile more as you serve others.

CHAPTER FIVE

Man the Walls!

With malice toward none; with charity for all;
with firmness in the right, as God gives us to see the right—
let us strive on to finish the work we are in.

ABRAHAM LINCOLN

1. Review chapter five and find two things that would have been hard for you to do, even knowing that you were helping others.

_____

_____

_____

Have you ever had to sell candy door to door to raise money for your soccer team uniforms? Have you ever had to say good-bye to an older brother or sister who went into the army or air force? Thinking about these things will help you find your answers to the question above.

2. Mr. Franklin tackled the hard things he did to serve others in good ways. He didn't get upset or fight. Name two things that he did do.

_____

_____

STUCK? *Read the verse on the next page for a good clue.*

WHAT THE BIBLE SAYS

Read Ephesians 4:29
No rotten talk should come from your mouth,
but only what is good for the building up of someone in need,
in order to give grace to those who hear.

When you are trying to help someone in a hard situation, it's easy to get mad and let bad words slip out. God talks about this problem in the above verse. What does He mention at the end of the passage that can help us watch what we say?

IT'S YOUR TURN

Do you have a friend who gets picked on by others? Have you tried to help your friend by taking his side? Think about what you said. Reread the verse above. Ask God to show you how to help others in hard situations without saying the wrong things.

Turkey Shock

It will always do to be changed for the better.

JAMES THOMSON

1. In chapter six Ben Franklin is constantly trying to make things that could help others. He didn't always succeed. One time he even almost killed himself, but he kept on making stuff. Jot down what Mr. Franklin did that almost killed him.

_____

_____

It's hard to image life in the 1700s. If we want to cook something, we just turn a knob on the stove or press the microwave button. But none of these things existed when Ben Franklin lived.

2. Though he made mistakes, Mr. Franklin succeeded many times in making things that helped others. Name two of his helpful discoveries.

_____

_____

_____

_____

STUCK? *Think about cold winters!*

WHAT'S THE BIBLE SAYS

Read Romans 12:7, *New Living Translation*
If your gift is that of serving others, serve them well.
If you are a teacher, do a good job of teaching.

Not all of us are inventors like Ben Franklin. We can't come up with things to make that will help others. But God has made each one of us with abilities. In the verse above, God doesn't ask us to do what we cannot. But what does He ask us to do?

IT'S YOUR TURN

Think about some of the abilities that you have: playing a sport, playing a musical instrument, singing, writing, getting good grades, cleaning well. Now ask God to help you do your very best when you use these abilities to serve others.

A Flash of Lightning

It is better never to begin a good work than, having begun it, to stop.
VENERABLE BEDE

1. In chapter seven Ben Franklin finally gets to see some of his ideas used for helping the community. You'll find one idea that started on page 24 but wasn't finished until this chapter. Write down what that idea was.

_____

_____

2. Another helpful idea Mr. Franklin had kept the people of Philadelphia safer. Jot down this idea too.

_____

_____

Mr. Franklin had to be patient as he helped the people in his town. Many did not want the changes he suggested. But in time, they realized that Ben only wanted to serve them.

3. Benjamin Franklin liked to see things through. For years he experimented with electricity, trying to figure it out. He made many helpful discoveries about it, but what was his most famous?

_____

_____

STUCK? *Try flying a kite!*

W H A T   T H E   B I B L E   S A Y S

Read 2 Corinthians 8:11
But now finish the task as well,
that just as there was eagerness to desire it,
so there may also be a completion from what you have.

Sometimes the idea of helping another person looks great, and we dive right into it. But occasionally it doesn't turn out as we thought. What does this verse say about even the things we don't want to finish?

I T ' S   Y O U R   T U R N

Can you think about a helpful job that you did not complete? If you can, go back and finish it. If you can't think of one, ask the Lord to help you keep finishing the things that you start.

Colonel and Diplomat

Work as if you were to live a hundred years,
Pray as if you were to die tomorrow.
BENJAMIN FRANKLIN

1. Even as Ben Franklin got older, he did not stop serving the people around him. Write down three helpful things he did in this chapter, even though he was now almost fifty years old.

_____

_____

_____

Many of the helpful things that Mr. Franklin did in the 1700s are still used today, whether it's buying insurance or going to the hospital.

2. *From Settlement to City* ends when Benjamin Franklin was seventy years old, but he went on to serve our struggling new country until he died at eighty-four years of age. As a matter of fact, he is best known for his job during these later years of his life. What job did he do?

_____

_____

STUCK? *It's in the title of this chapter.*

W H A T   T H E   B I B L E   S A Y S

Read Romans 14:19
*So then, we must pursue what promotes peace
and what builds up one another.*

Ben Franklin is not the only one who needs to be a diplomat of peace. According to this verse, who else needs to serve by helping make peace between people?

I T ' S   Y O U R   T U R N

Is there someone you've fought with recently? If there is, pray about it and go to that person in an effort to serve by making peace.

Activities

From Settlement to City with Benjamin Franklin

The Ben Franklin Science Award

The city of Philadelphia is offering a science award that bears the name of its great citizen, Mr. Benjamin Franklin.

As Ben Franklin departs for England, seeking the best interests of our fair city, the community thought it fitting to honor him with a contest of scientific curiosity and imagination. All persons with a good mind and clear writing are encouraged to enter.

Enclosed you will find the instructions for a number of Ben Franklin's experiments. As you do them, you'll need to answer questions. Below each of your answers, there is one or more numbers. Find that number(s) on page 84. Write the letter from your answer in the space above the matching number. Each letter will provide a clue to the name of Mr. Franklin's latest invention. When you discover what it is, you will receive the Benjamin Franklin Science Award.

Example:

Clue answer e l e c t r i c i t y
                    7

Last page _ _ _ _   _ e _ _ _
           1 2 3 4   5 6 7 8 9 10

The Biologist

Do Ants Really Talk?

Biology is the science of life. The term did not exist in Ben Franklin's time. Before the 1800s, biology was considered two entirely different sciences: botany, the study of plants, and zoology, the study of animals. But as microscopes improved and scientists gathered more information about cells and molecules, they realized that animals and plants were similar and needed to be studied together.

Ben Franklin was fascinated by ants and believed that they could communicate. Try this experiment to find out if he was right.

What you need:
- A small jar or container that a string can be tied around
- A tree or bush limb away from your house that will support the weight of your jar
- 2 tablespoons of sugar
- 3 to 5 feet of string
- One ant

Directions:

1. *Put the 2 tablespoons of sugar into your jar or pot. Add a few drops of water to make the sugar into a syrup.*

2. *Tie the string securely to your jar or pot. Then tie your pot or jar to the tree or bush limb, being careful that it dangles in open space without touching anything.*

3. *Drop your one ant into the sugar pot and watch to see if it makes it out of the pot. When it crawls out, go do something else for a while.*

4. *One hour later come back and look at your pot again.*

Record your results:

Did the ant make it out of your pot?

When you returned after an hour, what did you find?

Ants Are Strong!

From the largest ant, which is an inch long, to the smallest one, which is the size of the letter i without the dot, these hard-working insects can carry loads many times their weight. To get an idea of what this means, think of four friends who weigh about the same as you do. Now imagine trying to pick all of them up at once!

A nts can't speak English or Spanish, but they do communicate. Look in the back of this book at the *"Did You Know?"* section. Find out the two ways that ants "talk."

__ __ __ __ __ and releasing
   5

— — — — — — — — — —
                    12

The Mathematician

Ben Franklin's Most Magic Square

Ben Franklin wasn't alone in his fascination with numbers. By the time he made his magic squares, people had been doing math for 4,000 years! Scientists have found ancient Babylonian, Egyptian, and Greek math figures. Discover the magic for yourself in Ben's intriguing mathematical puzzle.

Here are some things to try:

1. Add any horizontal row of numbers, or any vertical row, and the total will be 260.

2. Add the four corner numbers and the four numbers at the center of the square. They also total _____.

3. From any corner start adding the numbers diagonally toward the center and then, on the same side of the square, back out toward the opposite corner. (Example: 52, 3, 5, 54, 43, 28, 30, 45) They will also total _____ !

M r. Franklin was not the only person to make "magic squares." Look in the *"Did You Know?"* section in the back of this book and write down who else made them.

___ ___ ___ ___ ___ ___ ___ ___
3   9

52	61	4	13	20	29	36	45
14	3	62	51	46	35	30	19
53	60	5	12	21	28	37	44
11	6	59	54	43	38	27	22
55	58	7	10	23	26	39	42
9	8	57	56	41	40	25	24
50	63	2	15	18	31	34	47
16	1	64	49	48	33	32	17

The Scientist

Ben Franklin did his experiments at his home. Little is known about the actual room or shop, but it undoubtedly resembled a workshop more than a scientific laboratory.

An Electric Handshake

Ben Franklin was intrigued with electricity. He did many experiments to learn about it, including flying a kite in a thunderstorm. He wrote down much information about it, thought of many ways to use it, and then created the devices that put it to work. You can learn about the power of electricity in the simple experiments below.

An Electric Handshake

Franklin's Electrostatic Machine was a simple glass tube or rod with a wire wrapped around it. A silk scarf was pulled through it or wool cloth was rubbed on it to produce static electricity. Just as he used it to create an "electric kiss," you can create an electric handshake.

What to do:

1. Put on a pair of slick-bottom dress shoes and rub them back and forth over a nylon carpet.

2. Then offer to shake hands with someone. You will both get a shock.

What happened:

The static electricity created by the friction between your shoes and the rug was picked up by your body. When you touched the other person, the electricity jumped from your body to theirs, causing the brief shock.

See the Power of Static Electricity

You can't see with your eyes how things are charged, but you can see their power to attract or repel. Try these experiments to see the power at work.

What you need:
- *Plastic comb*
- *Wool sock or coat sleeve*
- *Ping-Pong ball*
- *Salt and pepper*
- *Water faucet*

Try the following:

Experiment #1:
1. *Rub the comb with the wool to charge it with static electricity.*
2. *Put the Ping-Pong ball on a flat surface and hold the comb a few inches away.*
3. *Watch the ball roll toward the comb.*

Experiment #2:
1. *Rub the comb with the wool to charge it with static electricity.*
2. *Mix a few salt and pepper grains in a dish.*
3. *Hold the comb just above the dish and watch it pull the pepper grains out.*

Experiment #3:
1. *Rub the comb with the wool to charge it with static electricity.*
2. *Start a small stream of water running from a faucet.*
3. *Hold the comb next to the stream of water and watch it bend toward the comb.*

I n experiment #2, what was attracted by the charged comb?

— — — — — —
13

Electric Batteries

After a while, Ben realized that static electricity could only do so much. To make this new energy really useful, it needed to be more powerful. When he saw Leyden's jar battery, he improved it but not without danger. The more electricity he stored, the more powerful the shocks. Some of his experiments were very dangerous, and the electric blow he got while trying to cook his Christmas turkey could have killed him.

Dangerous Electric Kite

Flying a kite with a metal rod attached to it in a storm is very dangerous and should never be tried. Ben Franklin and his son were very lucky that their silk thread did not get wet in the rain. Since water conducts electricity, if it had been wet, whoever was holding the string would have taken the full charge of the lightning. In 1753 Professor George Richmann flew a kite, and the string got wet. He died from the electrocution.

The Physicist

What's Hot and What's Not

A physicist studies the basic parts of the universe (water, wind, rocks, light, etc.), the forces they exert on each other, and the results. An example would be studying how water cuts into rock, creating valleys and caves. In the experiments below you'll discover how wind affects water and how colors affect heat.

Oil and Water

When Ben Franklin took walks, he often brought a small bottle of oil with him. He studied how water and oil reacted to each other and eventually figured out that oil could calm waves in water.

What you need:

* *A 9 x13 pan with a couple of inches of water in it*
* *A fan powerful enough to ripple the water*
* *A small amount of oil*

How to do it:

1. *Set up the fan and pan of water, so that when turned on, the fan causes the water to ripple.*
2. *Pour a small amount of oil into the water, and watch the ripples disappear.*

What happened:

Ben Franklin discovered that wind would "catch" on the water, causing it to ripple. But when oil was poured on the water, it made the surface slick, and the wind couldn't "catch" it.

Other Water Discoveries

As Ben Franklin sailed back and forth to England, he noticed that it took many more days to sail from England to America than to sail from America to England. This caused him to talk with whaling ship captains, and they told him about a fast current in the Atlantic Ocean. He set out to chart it, finding that it was warmer than the regular ocean water. When finished, Ben called the current the Gulf Stream.

Learn about Colors and Heat

What you need:
- *A sunny day*
- *Small pieces of different-colored material (Make sure you have a variety of light and dark colors.)*
- *Snow or the same number of ice cubes as you have pieces of fabric*

Directions:
1. *If you have snow, find a clean, undisturbed patch in a sunny spot. If you don't have snow, find a sunny spot on your deck, driveway, or sidewalk that does not get in people's way.*
2. *If you have snow, lay the pieces of fabric on top of the spot you selected. If you don't have snow, put ice cubes in your selected spot and lay a piece of fabric on top of each one.*
3. *If you have snow, check every fifteen minutes to see how quickly it is melting under each piece of colored fabric. If you don't have snow, check every five minutes to see how quickly the ice cubes melt under each piece of colored fabric.*

Record your answer:
Under which color did the snow or ice cube melt the fastest? (Check back on page 32 to see if your answer matches Ben Franklin's.)

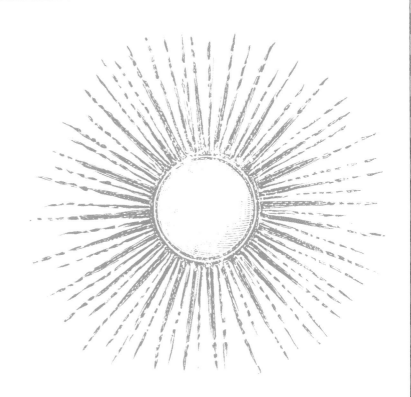

This experiment shows you which colors soak up heat and which colors bounce heat off of them. Based on this, on a cold day, what is the best color you can wear to keep warm?

_____ _____ _____ _____
 1   10

The Linguist

Having Fun with Words

Besides making magic squares, Benjamin Franklin also made rebuses. These are written messages that do not use just letters to communicate. Instead pictures, numbers, and the placement of words make up part of the message. See if you can figure out some of these word puzzles, then try to come up with some of your own.

Franklin the Linguist
Ben Franklin studied many languages. He taught himself how to speak and read English, Italian, Spanish, and Latin.

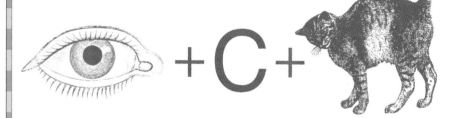

1. *A picture of an eye followed by the letter "C" and a picture of a cat = "I see a cat."*

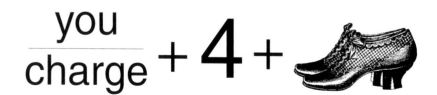

2. *"You overcharge for shoes."*

Can You Read This?

U put a  in my

I n another kind of word game, Ben Franklin used a word that had two meanings. Look on pages 28 of this book and see if you can find the double-meaning word that got the Quakers to approve the purchase of gunpowder.

— — — — — — —
8   11

Below is a section of the rebus that Ben called "The Art of Making Money Plenty." Americans 200 years ago talked differently than we do today—so it could take a little work to figure this one out.

Now You Try:

Make your own rebus for this sentence:

I want you to buy birdseed and a sack of flour.

The Inventor

From Bifocals to Woodstoves

Ben Franklin invented a lot of things because he often asked, "Why does it do that?" and "How does that work?" Curiosity and an interest in things around him caused Ben to see what many others didn't. Here are a few of the things Ben Franklin invented.

Bifocals

Franklin came up with the idea for bifocals at a dinner party. Although he could see his guests when he used his regular glasses, he was frustrated because he could not see the food on his plate without putting on his reading glasses. So he invented bifocals—spectacles in which the bottom is for reading and the top is for seeing far distances.

Lightning Rod

For years people saw lightning strike trees and homes, causing them to catch on fire. But no one knew how to protect his house. When Ben Franklin flew his kite in the storm, he realized that metal attracted lightning bolts. Since metal didn't catch fire like wood, he figured out that if a metal rod was put on a house, the lightning would strike it, leaving the house undamaged.

SOME OTHER FAMOUS INVENTORS INCLUDE:	
Alexander Graham Bell Telephone	Isaac Newton Ridges on coin edges (to keep people from shaving off gold or silver)
Jack St. Clair Kilby Microchip (basis of computers)	
	Galileo Galilei Improved telescope

Table-top Chair

If kids in school don't sit at a table or desk, they sit in a chair that has a writing table attached to its arm. The small table swings out of the way, so the person can get in and out of the chair. Ben Franklin invented this chair in the middle of the 1700s, and it has been used ever since!

Besides inventing practical things, Ben Franklin also invented a musical instrument that used spinning glass bowls in water. Look in the "Did You Know?" section on page 81 and find out what Franklin called his instrument.

___ ___ ___ ___ ___ ___ ___ ___

        4   6

What's left to be invented?

Can you think of three things that haven't been invented?

Odometer

Since Ben knew how many feet were in a mile and how many feet went around a carriage wheel, he thought there should be a way to measure distance without needing to step it off. In the end he made a box containing three connecting wheels that measured off feet and miles when attached to the wheel of a carriage.

Franklin Woodstove

For years the only warmth in homes was a fireplace. Often these didn't heat well and were smoky. As Franklin studied the action of air currents when cold air and warm air collided, he figured out a way to make chimneys "draw" out the smoke better. He also realized that metal held heat much longer than wood. From these two insights, he built the first wood-burning stove. The Franklin Stove is still made today.

The Printer

In Black and White

Today newspapers and books are run on huge presses powered by electricity. But when Ben Franklin was taught the printing trade by his older brother, everything was done by hand. Let's learn how printing progressed through the years.

Movable-type Printing Press
To avoid recarving every time another page needed to be printed, men began thinking of making separate letters and numbers that could be arranged to spell out one page and then rearranged to spell out another. Carved wood soon lost its edge and eventually letter molds were made and hot metal poured into them. The metal letters and numbers were held in order by frames. After inking the metal letters, a piece of paper was pressed on the type. In 1450 Johannes Gutenberg was one of the first printers to use "movable type." He printed the Holy Bible. Forty-seven copies of this early printed Bible still exist today throughout the world. One of the finest copies remaining is in the United States Library of Congress.

By Hand
Before printing presses were invented, everything was copied by hand. Scholars and religious monks spent days copying books. For this reason it was expensive to buy books, and poor people rarely owned one.

Printing Blocks or Presses
The next step in developing printing came with "engravers." These people carved words and/or pictures on the top of blocks of wood and called them "wood cuts." After finishing what they wanted printed, engravers brushed the carved wood with ink. Then they pressed a piece of paper on its surface. Afterward, they carefully peeled off the paper and allowed the "printed" work to dry. Carving took lots of time, and people often smeared the printing while trying to peel the paper off the block. People still couldn't get books easily.

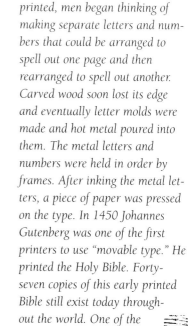

On page 27 of this book you read about a pamphlet that Ben Franklin printed on his press. What was the name of it?

— — — — —
7

— — — — —

Franklin's Press

Franklin's press was made of wood. Since electricity's power was still not controlled for practical use, an "arm" needed to be pulled down by hand to make a top block come down and press the paper onto the inked blocks.

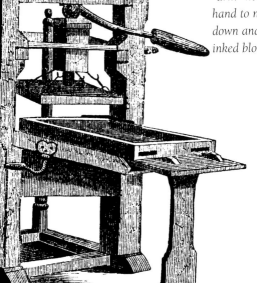

Printing Developments

Printing presses improved in many ways. Some of these include:

1. *A better system to hold the type together*
2. *A better system to run the paper through the press*
3. *Electricity to power the press's movements*

Make Your Own Printing Press

What you need:

(You will be using a knife, so ask for your parents' permission and help.)
- *A small potato*
- *Food coloring*

What to do:

1. *Slice the potato in half the long way and use a marker to write a letter on its flat surface. (Remember: Letters must be drawn backwards, so start with simple letters such as L or H.)*

2. *Cut away the potato around the letter. Then carefully cut along the letter's edges.*

3. *Put a small amount of food coloring into a dish. Press your potato letter into the coloring and then "print" it on some paper.*

The Civil Servant

From Fireman to Postman

At first people didn't know what to think about Ben Franklin, who always wanted to change things. But after a while they realized he wanted to make Philadelphia a better place to live. He volunteered for many colony jobs that paid little or no money in order to help. From firefighter to militia leader, Ben put his time and energy into helping his fellow citizens.

Militia Leader

Ben Franklin's interests did not really include the military, but he was not a man to see a need and turn his back. When Philadelphia was threatened, he did what needed to be done. He argued in the Assembly to get arms and supplies. He traveled to get cannons from other colonies. He helped get men to train and fight, and he fought in actual battles. Ben helped protect Philadelphia in the French and Indian War.

Firefighter

When we look at pictures of Ben Franklin in books, it is hard to imagine the pudgy man with wire-rim glasses fighting fires, but don't be fooled! Ben loved water, and as a young man, he swam regularly. He even won some races. He hauled leather buckets with the other firefighters and helped save many homes.

Assembly Recorder

I have little doubt that Ben would have preferred to experiment with electricity than to listen to politicians talk and argue. But as recorder for the Pennsylvania Assembly, he learned things that later helped our country. When he became a diplomat to England and France, he knew how political leaders acted and spoke. He knew what it took to settle arguments and when to stop giving in to demands. As a result, he helped to write our country's first two foreign treaties.

Postmaster

In Ben's day no one complained if the mail was slow—they were surprised and excited if they even got a letter! But while others accepted the situation, Ben saw how it could be improved and took on the job. His ideas of creating mail houses (post offices) and mail routes is still the foundation of our mail system today.

Today the men and women who bring our mail to us are called mail carriers. But when our country was still thirteen colonies, letters were carried by ship, travelers, and people hired to go between major settlements. Look back on page 20 and write down what their first hired "mail carriers" were called.

— — — — —
14

— — — — — —
2

Go to page 84 to decode the message.

A candle maker pouring wax into molds

Ants

Ants are social insects that live in organized colonies. More than 4,500 different types live throughout the world, and all of them can communicate with each other. Though they sometimes talk by touch, ants "tell" other ants about finding food by discharging a chemical that can be traced back to the food. The larger the supply of food found, the more chemical is released.

Apprenticeship

Apprenticeship was a system of training. An apprentice worked beside a skilled craftsperson to learn how to do his or her job. In exchange for the training, the apprentice agreed to work for the craftsperson for a specified number of years. From printing to blacksmithing, skills were passed from person to person under this system.

Cotillion dancers

Books

Before people made books, they used clay tablets. Then they made scrolls by rolling up long pieces of "papyrus paper" made from the pithy insides of reeds along the Nile River. But the paper didn't last long, so many scroll makers used strips of tanned animal hides. It wasn't until 1,500 years ago that the Romans and Greeks used rings to hold together sheets of wood, skins, and papyrus. They called this first book a codex.

Edward Braddock

During the French and Indian War, this British general was foolish not to guard against Indian ambush, but he did not lack for bravery. He was wounded in a battle with the Indians in which four horses were shot out from under him. Before dying of his wounds, the general valiantly fought back even as three-fourths of his men died around him.

Candle Making

For years candles were made by repeatedly dipping cotton wicks into hot wax or fat. Once dipped, the candles dried and then were dipped again. This was repeated until the candle got as thick as desired. Today most candles are molded by machines.

Cotillion

This dance started in France in the early 1700s. Four couples formed a square and did fancy steps while facing each other. It became popular and spread to England and North America. When it came to our country, we added more patterns and partner exchanges and gave it a new name—square dancing.

Did you

Cricket

This complicated game has eleven players on each team. A paddle-shaped bat is used to hit a ball that is smaller than a baseball. Players "bowl" the ball while opposing "batmen" try to hit it into the other team's goal. It is the national game of England and is also popular in other countries such as New Zealand, Australia, South Africa, and Zimbabwe.

Delawares

These Indians were among the first people early Americans met in the New World. The English called them Delawares because they lived along the Delaware River, but the tribe called themselves Leni-Lenape, which means "original people." They were respected by many other tribes, and Delaware braves were often referred to as "grandfather." Pushed west by settlers, descendants of this tribe now live in Canada and Oklahoma.

Firefighting

Even after bucket brigades were organized and fire hoses and water pumpers were invented, most towns in America continued to endure major fires. After a terrible fire ran through the city of Chicago in 1871, destroying 17,500 buildings and killing 300 people, towns passed laws to prohibit buildings being built so close together so that fires did not spread so easily.

The French and Indian War

This was the last of four wars fought to determine who would control America. This war lasted nine years, with the French winning most of the battles at first, primarily because England treated the colonists like low-class people. When the British changed their attitude toward us, the colonists increased their support of England's efforts. The result was that England won the war, and the French lost their hold in the New World.

George Handel

This German musician wrote his first opera when he was only nineteen years old. It became popular throughout the Western world, and soon he was studying and writing music in Italy and England as well as Germany. Though not everyone likes classical music, most people today have heard parts of his Messiah. Its "Hallelujah Chorus" is especially well-known.

Glass Armonica

Franklin finished creating this musical instrument in 1762. It had thirty-seven glass bowls that spun around in a case full of water. When a person touched the wet rims, they produced soft, warbling sounds. Two famous composers, Mozart and Beethoven, wrote music for this instrument.

Everything You Ever Wanted to Know about the Time of Benjamin Franklin

know?

Hooped Petticoat

This awkward undergarment was made of a whale-bone or spring-hoop frame that hung from a woman's waist in an inverted cone shape. Worn under the skirt, it made the dress widen down to the floor. At the height of their popularity, hoops could measure up to eighteen feet around. Ben Franklin wasn't the only one to despise them since they took up so much room in stagecoaches, around dinner tables, and elsewhere.

Hospitals

Hospitals have been around for a long time! Ancient people used their temples as refuges for sick and weak people, as well as places to train doctors. Later religious groups supported most hospitals. It wasn't until 1751, after Ben Franklin's fund-raising efforts, that the first publicly financed hospital opened.

Imagination

Imagination is the ability to think and suppose, often creating pictures in the mind. It is the basis for every invention, game, and book created. Ben Franklin had tons of it. Everything he saw was subject to his thoughts and "what ifs." Today many scientists believe that watching lots of television can take away a person's ability to imagine.

Immigrants

The United States has often been referred to as a "melting pot." This is because most Americans can trace their ancestors back to Germany, Ireland, Sweden, Mexico, Spain, France, England, etc. Except for native Indians, all Americans come from people who traveled here from another country and were at one time immigrants.

Indigo

This plant with purple, pink, or white flowers likes hot, wet weather. It was used to make a vibrant, deep-blue dye that was especially prized during the colonial era. Long before Eliza Pinckney grew specialized indigo plants that produced lots of seeds, Egyptians and Romans used indigo to make their own beautiful dye.

Iron

Iron is a common metal found in the earth, often giving dirt a brownish-red color. When not mixed with anything else, it is silvery white and soft; but when heated, it easily bonds with other elements. People have made it into decorations and weapons for thousands of years. Today it is used in wrought-iron furniture, fencing, and railings, and in the manufacture of steel and sheet metal.

Cricket player

Philadelphia in Ben Franklin's day

Kites

Long before Ben Franklin used kites to pull himself through the water and to test if lightning was electricity, ancient Chinese, Japanese, and Egyptian people flew kites. Nobody knows who built the first one or how it got its name, but there are also twenty-one types of birds that are called kites!

Libraries

There are many kinds of libraries besides public and school ones. Most large organizations such as hospitals, religious denominations, and business corporations have libraries too. Also many individual people collect books, creating personal libraries.

Magic Squares

As a clerk for the Pennsylvania Assembly, Ben Franklin had to listen to a lot of talk but couldn't speak himself. He often got bored and doodled, making magic squares. Though his were often exceptional, other people had made them before him. One man named Frenicle published more than eighty pages of them.

Malaria "Yellow Ghost"

This disease is caused by the bite of about sixty different types of mosquitoes, usually found in places with tropical weather such as Africa, South America, and places in Asia. When a person gets malaria, he experiences chills, high fevers, deliriums, and even comas. For years doctors treated malaria with quinine or manmade products similar to it. But with more than 100 million new cases of malaria reported every year, doctors are working on a vaccine that will prevent people from ever getting the disease.

William Penn

The founder of Pennsylvania was the son of an admiral who owned estates in England and Ireland. While being educated at Oxford, William learned and adopted the Quaker beliefs. Imprisoned in both Ireland and England for his faith, he knew firsthand of the need for a safe place to worship. So when the king of England gave him land in the New World to pay off a debt to his father, William established Pennsylvania.

Philadelphia

This sprawling metropolis is now the fifth largest city in the United States. More than five million people live in and around its 135 square miles. Its port is one of the busiest in the world, handling more than 5,000 cargo ships each year. When William Penn staked out this settlement, he could never have guessed how big it would grow!

Eliza Pinckney

Because Eliza's mother died early and her father was an officer in the British military, she ran the family's three South Carolina plantations when she was only sixteen years old. She was educated in England, and her training allowed her to study the plants she loved and help her colony. Later her sons played major roles in the American Revolution and in our nation's new government. Eliza was respected throughout the colonies, and George Washington helped carry her casket at her funeral.

German composer George Handel

Lucy Terry Prince

Phillis Wheatley is often thought to be our country's first African-American poet, but Lucy Terry Prince's poem was written twenty-one years before Wheatley's first one. Eventually Lucy was freed when a black man named Abijah Prince purchased and married her. However, when she tried to enroll her son in college, he was refused because of the color of his skin.

Plaster of Paris

Plaster of Paris is made from a mineral called gypsum. It is heated to remove some of its water, then ground up to make a powder. One form of plaster of Paris is mixed with water and molded or sculpted to make statues, false teeth, and ceramics. A second kind of plaster of Paris is used as fertilizer after some of its calcium content is reduced. This was what Ben Franklin used to plaster the farmer's field.

Post Office

After the American colonies declared their independence, the General Post Office in London no longer controlled America's mail. The Continental Congress elected Ben Franklin to create a postal system for the new country. Under his direction, seventy-five local post offices and 1,875 miles of postal routes were created. Today, post offices and postal routes are still key parts of our mail system.

Pounds

In England, a pound is an amount of money similar to our dollar. If you went to England today, you'd

An early post office

find it takes almost two American dollars to make one British pound. That means that William Penn's loss of money from owning Pennsylvania was almost $60,000!

Quakers

Quaker is a popular name given to people who belong to the Society of Friends. This religious group was started in the 1600s in England. Quakers believed that all people can be filled by God's Spirit and understand His Word. They tried to live simply and be truthful. They wanted churches kept separate from government and refused to pay tithes to the Church of England. This resulted in harsh treatment and caused William Penn to want to create a safe place for them in the New World.

Rubber

Long before Columbus brought this product back to Europe,

South American natives used rubber to make water-resistant coats, shoes, and capes. The Spanish tried to copy these products but failed, and for 200 years rubber was just a curiosity. Then in 1735 an expedition sent back to Europe rolls of crude rubber with descriptions of how the natives used it. From that point on scientists worked with the material. However, it didn't get its name until 1770 when a British chemist discovered it could rub away pencil marks.

Jonathan Swift

This famous English writer felt strongly about unfair and poor conditions in England. He used his writing to try to make changes in the government and expose the awful life of orphans and other people who were mistreated by society. His best-known work, *Gulliver's Travels,* has recently been made into a movie starring Ted Danson. Our story's fictional heroine, Suzanna Hale, named her cat after Swift's character, Gulliver.

University of Pennsylvania

This school of higher education that Ben Franklin started now trains more than 22,000 students! Its 260-acre campus is still located in Philadelphia, and its students can earn degrees in everything from architecture to veterinary medicine.

George Whitefield

This evangelist was an ordained priest in the Church of England, but his unconventional preaching caused many churches to refuse to let him preach from their pulpits. So he began preaching in the open air, attracting huge crowds in England, Scotland, Wales, and America. He worked with Jonathan Edwards in starting a revival in America called the "Great Awakening."

Wigs

Men began wearing wigs in the late 1600s. The fashion started when Louis XIV wore wigs to hide the fact that he was going bald. For more than 100 years, gentlemen wore white or gray wigs in large and fancy or small and simple styles. Even after the fashion died out, wigs were worn at royal activities. In fact, wigs are still worn by judges in the law courts of Great Britain.

The University of Pennsylvania in 1843

Will You Earn the Science Award?

It's time to put your clues together and discover what Benjamin Franklin's latest invention is.

A Final Clue: Mr. Franklin is older now and this invention was very practical and helped him.

<u> </u> <u> </u> <u> </u> <u> </u> <u> </u> <u> </u> <u> </u>
1   2   3   4   5   6   7

<u> </u> <u> </u> <u> </u> <u> </u> <u> </u> <u> </u> <u> </u>
8   9 10 11 12 13 14

Congratulations!

You have earned the Benjamin Franklin Science Award and the title of Honorary Junior Scientist!

Answers to clues: *Touch and releasing chemicals, Friendle, Pepper, Black, Grains, Armonica, Plain truth, Postsriders,* Answer to Ben's latest invention: Bifocal glasses.